Mr Bickle
and the
GHOST

Stella Gurney
and Silvia Raga

Evans

Mr Bickle lived alone.

5

Almost.

He hated having a ghost.

It teased. "Stop!"

11

It crashed.
"Quiet!"

13

It sang (terribly).
"Please!"

15

It went too far.

"Right! Enough!" shouted
Mr Bickle.

The hoover sucked –
the ghost popped.

Peace at last.

23

Alone again.

25

Mr Bickle sighed.

He pulled.

"Welcome back," smiled Mr Bickle.

Why not try reading another Twisters book?